First published in Great Britain by HarperCollins Publishers in 2003

9 10
ISBN-13: 978-0-00-712314-8

HarperCollins Children's Books is a division of HarperCollins Publishers Ltd.

MICHAEL BOND

PADDINGTON
AND THE GRAND TOUR

illustrated by BOB ALLEY

HarperCollins *Children's Books*

One morning Paddington answered the door bell at number thirty-two Windsor Gardens and to his surprise he found his best friend, Mr Gruber, waiting outside.

"I've decided to treat myself to an outing, Mr Brown," he said, "and I was wondering if you would care to join me?"

Paddington was very excited. He always enjoyed his days out with Mr Gruber and he didn't need asking twice.

In no time at all he returned with his suitcase full of marmalade sandwiches ready for the journey along with Mrs Bird's umbrella in case it rained.

They hadn't gone very far when Paddington spotted a bench.
"Perhaps we ought to eat our sandwiches now,
Mr Gruber," he said. "If it rains they might get wet."
While they had stopped Mr Gruber showed Paddington
some photographs of the places he wanted to visit.

"I thought we might go on what's called a Hop On – Hop Off bus," said Mr Gruber.

"You can come and go as you like, so it's possible to see lots of different sights with only one ticket."

"I don't think I've ever been on one of those before," said Paddington as they went on their way. "It sounds very good value."

But as they turned a corner and Paddington saw the waiting bus he nearly fell over backwards with alarm, for part of the roof was missing.

"I think the driver must have gone under a low bridge by mistake!" he exclaimed.

Mr Gruber laughed. "Don't worry, Mr Brown. It's made that way so that the passengers have a good view of the sights. If you wait here and form a queue," he continued, "I'll get the tickets. Then we can make sure of seats in the front row."

"That's a good idea," said an Inspector. "The early bird catches the worm and I'm expecting a large party of assorted overseas visitors any moment now."

"Perhaps I can interest you in one of these booklets telling you all about the trip," said the Inspector. "It comes in lots of different languages."

Paddington was most impressed. "Thank you very much," he said. "I'd like one in Peruvian, please."

"Peruvian!" repeated the man. "I'm afraid we don't get much call for that."

"You don't get much call for it?" exclaimed Paddington. "Everybody speaks it in Darkest Peru. You don't even have to call out."

He gave the man a hard stare.

"Wait here," said the Inspector nervously. "I'll see what I can do."

No sooner had the Inspector disappeared than Paddington
saw a crowd approaching, so he raised Mrs Bird's umbrella
in case he had a job finding him again.

"I'm sorry we're late," panted the leader of the group.

"We got held up."

Paddington politely raised his hat. "That's all right," he began. "We can't all be early birds. I'm forming a que…"

Before he had time to say any more he found himself being pushed to one side as there was a mad scramble to board the bus.

QUEUE here for NEXT BUS

P.B.

LONDON

Paddington watched in dismay as everyone on the top
deck began fighting for the front seats.

"I wouldn't sit there if I were you," he called.
"There may still be some worms." But he was wasting
his breath, so he tried again. "Excuse me," he called.
Lifting one leg, he waved the umbrella. "It's a Hop On
bus and I'm afraid the two front seats upstairs are
reserved."

"Hold it, you guys!" The leader gave a loud blast
on his whistle. "You're supposed to hop everywhere,
OK? Pass it down the line."

"What happens now?" came a voice, when
everyone was settled.

Paddington considered the matter for a moment.
"I'm not sure," he replied. "I shall need to ask Mr
Gruber, but I think you look at the view, then
you hop off again."

"View?" wailed someone. "What view?"

Their voices were lost in the general commotion
as the leader blew several more blasts on his
whistle and issued fresh instructions.

"I came on this trip to see the sights," protested a lady as she staggered off the bus, "not become one!"

"I'm worn out," gasped another, collapsing into her husband's arms, "and we haven't been anywhere yet!"

A number of passers-by stopped to watch and several children joined in the fun.

Soon the whole pavement was alive with figures.
Paddington tried closing his eyes, but whenever
he opened them more people had arrived.

He was very relieved when he spied a familiar figure
pushing his way through the crowd towards him.

"Are you all right, Mr Brown?" called Mr Gruber.
"This place looks like a battlefield."

"It feels like one, Mr Gruber," said Paddington.
"I was trying to save our seats in the front row, but
I'm afraid I wasn't quick enough."

QUEUE
here for
NEXT BUS

"The Inspector gave me this booklet," said Mr
Gruber. "He said he's very sorry it's in English, but
he suggested we find somewhere quiet to read it until
the fuss had died down. There's a little café over there.
I'll hurry on ahead and reserve a table."

Mr Gruber hadn't gone very far before Paddington felt a spot of rain on the end of his nose, so he stopped to open the umbrella. Almost immediately he heard a whistle and a voice shouting, "Follow him, you guys! Don't let him out of your sight!"

Paddington hurried on his way as fast as his legs would carry him. Even so, he only just managed to reach the café ahead of the others.

"Quick, Mr Brown," hissed a voice from behind some potted plants. "Over here. There's some cocoa on its way."

"I should be careful with your sips, Mr Brown," warned Mr Gruber as the waitress arrived with two steaming mugs. "It looks very hot and they may give the game away."

"I don't know about my sips, Mr Gruber," gasped
Paddington, as the crowd burst through the door.
"I'm beginning to wish I'd brought my disguise
outfit."

"There you are!" cried the leader. "I've never known a Tour Captain so hard to keep up with."

"Tour Captain?" repeated Paddington.

"You were holding up your umbrella…" said the man. "That's what Tour Captains always do. It's so that people don't get lost."

"I'm not a Tour Captain," said Paddington, hotly. "I'm a bear."

"Never mind," said a man. "The exercise has done us all good.
I haven't felt so fit in years."

   And to show how pleased they were, everyone
dropped a coin or two into Paddington's
umbrella as they went past.

"Well," said Mr Gruber, when it was all quiet again. "What do you think of that, Mr Brown?"

"I think," said Paddington, "I might become a Tour Captain when I'm old enough. It seems a very good job for a rainy day. Especially if you have your own umbrella!"

The crowd fell silent as they took in the news.

"You mean we've been doing all that hopping around for nothing," complained one of the party. "I thought it was some quaint old English custom."

"What are we going to do now?" cried someone else. "We've missed our bus!"

Paddington looked out of the window at the rain and then at his booklet. "I think I've got an idea coming on," he announced.

After explaining what he had in mind, he waited for the others to settle down. Then, while Mr Gruber held up his pictures one by one, Paddington read from the booklet.

If the words didn't always match up with the pictures no one seemed to mind, and at the end, as the sun came out again, they all applauded.

"That was the best tour I've never been on," said someone amid general agreement.

"I didn't know Buckingham Palace was over 60 metres high," said a lady as the party began to leave.

"I'm afraid it got mixed up with Nelson's Column by mistake," explained Paddington. "It's a bit difficult with paws and I must have turned over two pages at once."